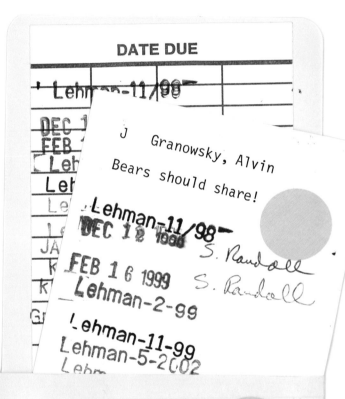

## Another Point of View

# Goldilocks and the Three Bears

retold by Dr. Alvin Granowsky
illustrations by Lyn Martin

STECK-VAUGHN
C O M P A N Y
ELEMENTARY • SECONDARY • ADULT • LIBRARY

 nce upon a time, there were three bears who lived in a little house in the woods. One of the bears was a cute, little baby bear. One was a middle-sized mama bear. One was a great big papa bear.

One day, the mama bear made a big pot of hot porridge. She poured the porridge into three bowls. Then she said, "Let's take a walk in the woods while our porridge cools."

So the three bears made their way down the path, deep into the woods.

The three bears weren't the only ones taking a walk in the woods. A pretty, little girl named Goldilocks had been picking flowers and had wandered far from home.

She came upon the three bears' cottage. "I wonder who lives in this little house," said Goldilocks.

She peeked in the window. "Is anyone home?" Goldilocks called. Then she knocked on the door. When no one answered, Goldilocks lifted the latch on the front door and walked into the little house.

Goldilocks was hungry from her walk in the woods. She saw three bowls on the table. "Oh, porridge!" she said. "I am so hungry, and it smells so good!"

First, she tasted the porridge in the big bowl. "This porridge is too hot," said Goldilocks.

Next, Goldilocks tasted the porridge in the middle-sized bowl. "This porridge is too cold," she said.

Then she tasted the porridge in the little bowl. "This porridge is just right," she said. So she ate it all up.

9

Goldilocks was tired from her long walk in the woods. She saw three chairs in a row. First, she sat upon the great big chair. "This chair is too hard," she said.

Next, she sat upon the middle-sized chair. "This chair is too soft," she said.

Then Goldilocks sat upon an itty-bitty chair. "This chair is just right," she said.

Goldilocks was happily rocking on that itty-bitty chair when suddenly it broke apart. "Dear me!" exclaimed Goldilocks as she fell to the floor.

Then Goldilocks felt very sleepy. She went upstairs to the bears' bedroom. First, she lay down on the great big bed. "This bed is too hard," she said.

Next, she lay down on the middle-sized bed. "This bed is too soft," she said.

Then Goldilocks lay down on the itty-bitty bed. "This bed is just right," she said. Goldilocks was so tired that just like that, she fell fast asleep.

While Goldilocks was sleeping, the three bears returned home.

"Somebody has been eating my porridge!" said the great big papa bear in his rough, gruff voice.

"Somebody has been eating my porridge!" said the middle-sized mama bear in her sweet, soft voice.

"Somebody has been eating my porridge," cried the cute, little baby bear in his itty-bitty voice. "And that somebody has eaten it all up!"

Then the great big papa bear took a look
at his chair. Its pillow was crooked.

"Somebody has been sitting on my chair!"
he said in his rough, gruff voice.

16

Then the middle-sized mama bear looked at her chair. Its pillow was all squished.

"Somebody has been sitting on my chair!" she said in her sweet, soft voice.

Then the cute, little baby bear looked at his chair. "Somebody has been sitting on my chair and has **broken** it all to pieces!" he said in his itty-bitty voice. He began to cry.

The three bears ran upstairs to see what
else had been done.

"Somebody has been lying on my bed!" said
the great big papa bear in his rough, gruff voice.

"Somebody has been lying on my bed!" said the middle-sized mama bear in her sweet, soft voice.

"Somebody has been lying on my bed!" said the cute, little baby bear in his itty-bitty voice. "And do you know what? She's still there!"

Goldilocks woke up, scared by the bears. She ran down the stairs, out the door, and away from that little house as fast as her legs would go.

And the three bears never ever saw Goldilocks again.

# BEARS SHOULD SHARE!

**Library of Congress Cataloging-in-Publication Data**

Granowsky, Alvin, 1936–
    Bears should share! / by Alvin Granowsky ; illustrations by Anne Lunsford. Goldilocks and the three bears / retold by Alvin Granowsky ; illustrations by Lyn Martin.
        p. cm. — (Another point of view)
    Titles from separate title pages; works issued back-to-back and inverted.
    Summary: Juxtaposes the traditional tale of the three bears' discovery that Goldilocks has been in their house eating their porridge and using their furniture with Goldilocks' side of the story.
    ISBN 0-8114-7127-6 — ISBN 0-8114-6634-5 (pbk.)
    1. Upside-down books—Specimens. [1. Folklore. 2. Bears—Folklore. 3. Upside-down books. 4. Toy and movable books.] I. Lunsford, Anne, ill. II. Martin, Lyn, ill. III. Granowsky, Alvin, 1936– Goldilocks and the three bears. 1996. IV. Title. V. Series.
PZ8.1.G735Be      1996
398.2—dc20                                                                95-9612
[E]                                                                          CIP
                                                                             AC

Printed and bound in the United States of America
1 2 3 4 5 6 7 8 9 00 LB 00 99 98 97 96 95

**Another Point of View**

# BEARS SHOULD SHARE!

by Dr. Alvin Granowsky

illustrations by Anne Lunsford

STECK-VAUGHN
C O M P A N Y
ELEMENTARY • SECONDARY • ADULT • LIBRARY

Don't ever listen to a little bear! I don't care how he might look at you with those big brown eyes. I'm telling you, he's making up a big story. Here's how I found out about cute little bears.

I was playing behind my house with my new ball. Then it just bounced off into the woods. When I went to get it, I saw the most darling little bear holding my ball. That little bear was so cute, I invited him to play ball with me. We had so much fun! When I had to leave, that cute little cub asked, "Will you come play with me at my house tomorrow?"

"Don't you have to ask your parents if it is all right?" I asked.

"Oh, no!" laughed the little cub. "My parents let me do whatever I want. Why don't you join us for breakfast? We might be on our morning walk when you get there. Just go on in and make yourself at home. You can do whatever you want."

"I could never go into a house when no one was there!" I said.

"It's fine with us bears," said the little cub. "After all, *bear* rhymes with *share*!"

"Well, isn't that nice? I'll be there in the morning," I said.

The cub told me how to get to his house. Then he walked off into the woods.

The next morning, I made my way to the bears' cottage. I knocked at the door, but no one answered. I called, "Hello! It's Goldilocks!" but no one answered. The cub had said I should go on in, so I did.

Three bowls of porridge were set out on
the kitchen table. "Can they all be for me?"
I wondered. Then I remembered the little bear's
words. "*Bear* rhymes with *share*," he had said.
"How kind of them!" I thought. So, I ate a bowl
of the porridge. It was just delicious. "I'll have
to compliment the bears on their cooking!"
I thought.

After eating, I went into the most charming little living room. Three chairs were lined up in a row. "*Bear* rhymes with *share*," I smiled to myself as I tried each chair. I found one I liked and sat there rocking. And then, *OOPS!* The chair broke. "Oh, well!" I said to myself. "When you share, sometimes things break."

It seemed to be taking a long time for the bears to get home. "What shall I do now?" I wondered. I decided to take a nap while waiting for the bears.

I went upstairs to lie down. I chose the most comfy bed they had and fell asleep.

The sounds of the bears coming home woke me up. I was looking forward to a wonderful day with my new friend and his parents.

But then I heard the papa bear say in his booming voice, "Why is our house unlocked? Little Bear, did you forget to lock the door again? We have told you how important it is to keep strangers out when we're not here!"

Then I heard Little Bear. He said, "You know I always obey you. I made sure the door was locked before we left. I know you and Mama don't want anyone in our house while we are out."

That wasn't what he had told me!

Then the bears noticed that I had eaten some of the porridge. "Someone's been eating my porridge," said Papa Bear in his booming voice. "I don't want anyone eating my porridge!"

"Someone's been eating my porridge," said Mama Bear in her quiet voice. "I don't want anyone eating my porridge!"

Then I heard Little Bear, the one I had *thought* was my friend. "Someone's been eating my porridge, and it's all gone!" he said in his baby bear voice.

I wondered what happened to "*Bear* rhymes with *share.*" It didn't sound like these bears were the sharing type. I got scared. I wasn't sure what to do next.

Then I heard the bears in the living room. "Somebody has been sitting on my chair," said Papa Bear in his booming voice. "I don't want anyone sitting on my chair!"

"Somebody has been sitting on my chair," said Mama Bear in her quiet voice. "I don't want anyone sitting on my chair!"

Then Little Bear began to fuss and cry. "Somebody has been sitting on my chair," he said in his baby bear voice. "Look! It's broken to pieces!"

Well, it was true. But as I said, sometimes things you share with others break. That's just the way it is.

Then I heard the bears coming up the stairs.
They came into the bedroom.

"Somebody has been sleeping on my bed!"
said Papa Bear in his booming voice. "I don't
want anyone sleeping on my bed!"

"Somebody has been sleeping on my bed!" said Mama Bear in her quiet voice. "I don't want anyone sleeping on my bed!"

"Somebody has been sleeping on my bed!" said Little Bear in his baby bear voice. "And she's still there!"

I looked up at that baby bear and gave him my sweetest smile. "Hi, Little Bear. Remember me? I'm your friend, Goldilocks, from down the path. Thanks for inviting me over. It was really sweet of you to leave the door unlocked. The porridge you left for me was just delicious. I appreciate it all."

"What?" asked Papa Bear in his booming voice.

"What?" asked Mama Bear in her quiet voice.

21

"Little Bear, have you been inviting strangers into our home while we're away?" asked Papa Bear. "You are in *BIG* trouble if that's what you've done!"

"But Papa, I've never seen this girl before in my life!" answered Little Bear.

That Little Bear was making up a great big story! I knew I had to get out of there fast.

"Thanks again for everything!" I called as I dashed down the stairs. I ran out of that house as fast as I could. I didn't stop until I was safely back home.

All I can say is that if you ever meet a bear cub, don't believe everything he says. If he says anything about *bear* rhyming with *share*, run away as fast as you can!

Listen to *my* rhyme instead—

*If you go visit that Little Bear,*
*You're sure to end up with a*
*GREAT BIG SCARE!*